Text and illustrations copyright 2020 by Mighty Fortress Press.

All rights reserved. Published by Mighty Fortress Press. No part of this book may be reproduced or transmitted in any form or by any means, electronic or mechanical, including photocopying, recording, or by any information storage and retrieval system, without written permission from the publisher.

For information, address:
Mighty Fortress Press
18411 Crenshaw Blvd. Suite 418
Torrance, California 90504.

For information about special discounts for bulk purchases, please contact Mighty Fortress Press sales at business@mightyfortresspress.com

First Edition, May 2020

Library of Congress Control Number: 2020906585

Kang, Eunice, author.
Yu, Jane, illustrator.
Kang, William, editor.
"A Mama What If Book"

ISBN-13: 978-1-7328644-3-6

Visit www.mightyfortresspress.com
Facebook: @mightyfortresspress
Instagram: @mightyfortresspress

Mama, What If?

Book 2: The Pirate Treasure

Written by
Eunice Kang

Illustrated by
Jane Yu

Wow!
A treasure map!

Many great explorers have used the magic hat to help them sail through rough waters for hundreds—no, thousands of years! And it can help you on your journey too!

Be strong and courageous. Do not be afraid. For the Lord your God will be with you wherever you go.

Joshua 1:9

Be strong and courageous. Do not be afraid. For the Lord your God will be with you wherever you go.

Joshua 1:9

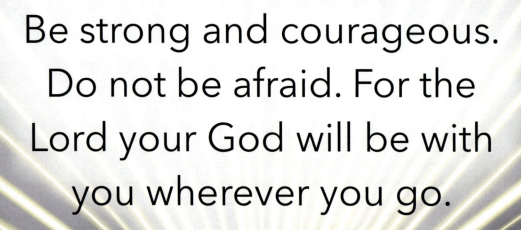

Be strong and courageous. Do not be afraid. For the Lord your God will be with you wherever you go.

Joshua 1:9

Be strong and courageous. Do not be afraid. For the Lord your God will be with you wherever you go.

Joshua 1:9

YES!

Be strong and courageous. Do not be afraid. For the Lord your God will be with you wherever you go.

Joshua 1:9

A Note from the Author

Before I went on my first missions trip to India during college, my mom gifted me a bookmark with a Bible verse written on it. I was scared to embark on a month-long journey, but this verse gave me courage and strength. I only wish that my mom had introduced this verse to me sooner!

That's why I wrote this book for readers like you! Hopefully, you will treasure this Bible verse deep in your heart at a young age and let it empower you for the rest of your life. So whenever you encounter challenges and obstacles, you can be guided by God's truth to navigate the right path. You can know that you are safe and secure in a relationship with a loving God who gives strength, courage, and peace.

Happy Reading!